SHADOWLAND
TALES
Of Magic & Mystery

A.P. SIMMONS

Copyright © 2021
A.P. Simmons
Shadowland Tales
Of History
All rights reserved.

No part of this publication may be reproduced, distributed, or transmitted in any form or by any means, including photocopying, recording, or other electronic or mechanical methods, without the prior written permission of the publisher, except in the case of brief quotations embodied in critical reviews and certain other non-commercial uses permitted by copyright law.

A.P. Simmons

Printed in the United States of America
First Printing 2021
First Edition 2021

ISBN 9798739428974

Edited By: Amyvwrite of Fiverr
Cover Design By: Germancreative of Fiverr

Designations used by companies to distinguish their products are often claimed as trademarks. All brand names and product names used in this book and on its cover are trade names, service marks, trademarks, and registered trademarks of their respective owners. The publishers and the book are not associated with any product or vendor mentioned in this book. None of the companies referenced within the book have endorsed the book.

acknowledgments

Thank you for taking the time to read this book. As an avid reader myself, I approach this book with a sense of responsibility.

I owe a great debt of gratitude to my primary editor, who you can find on Fiverr: amyvwrite. I also want to give thanks to the cover artist, who you can also find on Fiverr: German-creative, who saved me from some of my odd cover concepts.

SHADOWLAND

"Yea, though I walk through the valley of the shadow of death, I will fear no evil: for thou art with me."

Psalm of David, chapter 23, verse 4

Table of Contents

Old Medicine 1

Leave Well Enough Alone 11

Step On a Crack 21

James Creek Bridge 33

Bottom Feeder 47

Dream Amulet 51

Old Medicine

They tell us that the unexplored jungles and oceans of the world possess medicinal riches that can cure countless diseases and ailments. That is proving to be true, it appears. But what about the opposite? Are we releasing some things best left undiscovered? Do we even know it when it happens? In this tale we examine the idea that there may be two sides to the natural medicine coin.

May 1897

After years of work, Doctor Karl Shephard breathed a sigh of relief. His grant was approved. The team was secured. Permits were in order. The schedule was set.

Karl was a biologist at the College of St. Michael, a small but well-regarded college, particularly in the world of medicine. Karl and his team would be traveling to a rainforest in central Brazil, looking for a legendary rare plant. The plant was rumored to have the ability to extend life hundreds of years. This had been the rumor at least since the time of the Conquistadors.

Karl and his team did not take the legend literally, but he also knew most legends were based in part on facts. A plant having any anti-aging or healing properties would be worth a fortune. Not a fortune for Karl but it would certainly secure him grants into the foreseeable future, along with public regard and excellent job security.

~~~

June 1898

Travel into the Brazilian rainforest in 1898 was nothing like it would be today. There was no rail or road infrastructure reaching their destination. As with most expeditions of this type, they traveled by steamship to the inland city of Manaus. This was the golden age for the city. The Amazon rubber boom was in full swing.

After arriving and a night of sleep, Doctor Shephard assembled the primary team in the hotel for a briefing.

"I realize most of you have gotten to know each other on our trip up the river, but I wanted to take a little time to reaffirm everyone's roles and answer any questions before we begin next week."

Karl proceeded to introduce the primary team members and their roles. Doctor Paul Clausen was the team chemist. He was roughly 40 years old and a fellow faculty member at the College of St. Michael. Stanley Morgan was Karl's young graduate assistant. Elliot McFarsen was the representative of Bayern Chemical, the primary beneficiary of the grant making the trip possible. He was in his late 30s and rumored to be a son of one of the board members. Francisco Santos was the Brazilian in charge of security, the porters, and securing supplies. Francisco was a man in his late 40s and would best be described as a disciplined former army officer for Brazil. He was a veteran of the War of Oranges, where Portugal and Brazil defeated France and Spain.

"Very well, gentlemen. Do you have any questions for me at this time?" asked Karl.

Paul Clausen was the first. "Dr. Shephard..."

"Please, call me Karl."

"Karl, how far from Manaus before we reach the target region?"

"Ah, yes. I realize I was a bit vague in your preliminary brief. At the time, I wasn't sure how far our supply line would allow us to proceed from here. But now that we are here, Mr. Santos assures me we will be able to proceed 200-250 miles into the northwestern forest. Assuming we need to go that far, of course."

Elliot McFarsen was next. "I have a question for Mr. Santos. Sir, what weight do the locals place on the rumor of the plant we seek?"

Francisco was bilingual but spoke with a heavy accent.

"Mr. McFarsen, this is just one of many legends that come from the time of the Conquistadors. I believe your typical locals neither believe nor disbelieve these stories. They know the forest is a mysterious place full of wonders."

After some more discussion and a toast, the party broke up for the evening.

Four days later, they took a boat to the west bank of the Rio Negro and began their expedition. Francisco stayed toward the front of the column. This way he could direct the scouts and pathfinders most efficiently.

A planned rhythm quickly established itself. The party would travel 10-15 miles and set up camp. At that point, the native workers would fan out and collect plant specimens based on instructions from Dr. Shephard. Dr. Clausen oversaw the chemical analysis of the promising samples. This would proceed for 2-3 days, at which point they would pack up and repeat the process. Days stretched into weeks. One evening the two doctors discussed findings around a campfire before going to sleep. It was a daily habit.

Paul Clausen puffed on his pipe and posed a question. "Karl, have you noticed the natives are not going so far from camp as we get farther into the forest?"

"Francisco said they are a bit nervous about hostile tribes and jaguars. He doesn't think it will pose a major issue," Karl replied.

"Very well. I may venture out some with them to brace their spirits a bit. Also, I had a positive result with a sample I tested today," said Paul, puffing on his pipe.

"You don't say? So, what did you observe?"

"Well, one of the natives brought in a plant sample. From what I could make of it, he said that his grandmother used to use it in a diluted mixture for severe injuries. I decided to test it on one of the lame mules, and I have to say it seemed to have an immediate curative effect on his damaged hoof."

"That's great news! We haven't had much to celebrate so far," said Karl.

Paul chuckled and tamped out his pipe. He rose and said, "Well, Karl, I'm not ready to tell Elliot to prepare a telegraph just yet."

They retired for the night in good spirits.

Several days later, Karl was surprised when Dr. Clausen was brought back to camp being carried by several scared natives. He was unconscious and had a severely broken leg as well as a terrible bruising on his back. While Karl attended to Paul, Francisco got the story from the natives about what had happened.

"Dr. Shephard, they told me Dr. Clausen took a fall while trying to retrieve a specimen from a tree. They said he landed on tree roots, which is why his injuries are great," explained Francisco.

"Good Lord. Francisco, you are our field surgeon. Can you set his leg?" asked Karl.

"Doctor, you and I both know that leg is broken in several places. And we do not know how severe his back injuries are yet. I think, for now, we make him comfortable. This may exceed our abilities. And I know of no medicine that could help him."

Francisco's comment gave Karl an idea. "Francisco, stay with him. Paul had discovered a plant that just may be able to help him. I'll go get it."

An hour later, Karl had retrieved and applied the medicine. He did not know how to dilute the plant, so he ground it up, mixed in some water, and created a poultice to apply to Paul's wounds. Paul was breathing evenly now. While still unconscious, his color was better and was apparently helping him to heal. But was it enough?

Miraculously, Paul lived through the night. He was awake and speaking. He did not appear to be in much pain.

"Dr. Paul Clausen! You gave us a mighty scare! We thought you were on death's door when it occurred to me that you may have discovered your own cure!" exclaimed Karl.

"Dr. Shephard is right," said Francisco. "We feared the worst for you."

Paul was tired but in decent spirits. "Well fellows, I appear to owe all of you my life. I guess I'll have to take your word about my injuries, but I can assure you that as of now, I believe I am doing pretty well considering the fall I took."

"Let's have a look at that leg and your back," said Francisco.

Francisco examined Paul's leg and back. While his body and bones appeared sound, they also appeared to have scab-like growths—*scales?*—where the poultice had been applied. Francisco knew wounds from his time in the army, and this did not look normal. On the other hand, he was no professionally trained Doctor of Medicine, and this may be a side effect of the plant. For now, he kept his thoughts to himself.

The next day, Paul insisted on getting out of the bed and returning to his duties, which would now focus on the plant that had apparently saved him. He said he had never felt better. His wounds did not show with his normal clothing on. This was welcome news, but it also brought about consternation with the natives. Several of them had retrieved Dr. Clausen and knew there was no natural way for him to have recovered this quickly. It was serious enough that Francisco called a meeting with them at the end of the day to discuss it. He explained how their expedition was here to find a plant with these properties, and they very well may have succeeded! There was nothing supernatural about Dr. Clausen's recovery.

This had the desired effect. The rumblings of discontent quieted down.

Until the next day.

Dr. Clausen's scaly skin was getting worse and spreading. Most of his face was displaying the scaled appearance. The gait of his walk was changing. His legs were changing. All of that might have been explained away, but the emergence of two knobby growths on the top of Clausen's head were taken as a clear sign of the devil and would not be explained away.

Dr. Paul Clausen left a note that evening and disappeared. Karl, Francisco, and Elliot met to read it and discuss what to do.

"Gentlemen, allow me to read the note—it is brief," said Karl.

Karl, my presence is a detriment to the party. We both know why and that there is nothing to be done. I will retreat into the jungle and try to find my own way out. It is clear we found our target plant, but now we know why it has remained obscured. I am healed, but I am transforming into something people will not understand or tolerate. If I can make it to civilization, perhaps I can get treatment. Otherwise, I thank you for your friendship and wish you and the party the blessings of our Lord.

Karl said nothing further and handed the note to Elliot. All three of the men were moved.

"Well, I believe the right thing to do is to wait a day or two and then start back to Manaus," said Elliot. No one argued. He continued, "We have secured several interesting specimens. I have to believe that the company will get a return on their expenditures, and I will make sure Paul gets his due credit."

That is what they did. The retreat to Manaus was without major problems, and a few more promising plant samples were taken. The expedition then sailed down to the port of Belém, where passage back to the United States was secured. The expedition was considered a minor success by the business and academic partners.

~~~

May 2018

Dr. Jennie Olsen was leading the small team of scientists into the Brazilian rainforest. Like her colleagues, she had read many of the books about the early 20th century expeditions. Jennie was an employee of a major bio pharmaceutical company along with the other party members. Her party was camped for the night and were circled around the fire.

"It's hard to imagine being here a century or more ago. It was so much more isolated. Wild," stated Jennie.

Dr. Kalif Davar, a junior member agreed, "Yes, can you imagine all the mules and natives and the size of such a group?"

Research graduate assistant Charles VanHaven added, "I think, for me, it would weigh on me that there would be no help if something serious went wrong. No phones or helicopters could come get you."

The group chatted amiably for a bit longer before retiring to bed for the night.

Just outside the range of the firelight was an observer. He heard every word the group had spoken. He was an apex predator here. His hide was generally scaled and extremely tough but flexible. His shoulders and upper back were swollen with powerful muscle groups. His arms were long enough to touch the ground with little effort. Powerful hands, almost claw-like, were at their ends.

He was a solitary creature. He considered himself a guardian. His name had been Dr. Paul Clausen when he had mingled with men so long ago, but his memory was clear. And he would do everything possible to ensure the plant that could provide longevity remained safely undiscovered.

Leave Well Enough Alone

We owe so much to our teachers. Well, to most of them. After all, they are a cross-section of our society and within that diversity there are some outliers. Some for the better, some for the worse. In this tale we peek into the secretive world of students. The world they do not want to share with adults. After all, would we believe them?

David and Andrew were good friends. They were in the 9th grade and enduring their first year of high school as male freshmen, the lowest of the low.

They had met in middle school and been fast friends, in no small part due to their unique senses of humor. They were discreet. Smart. But irreverent.

One of their favorite past times was to use a communication system based on noises in the classroom. Innocuous noise. Noises that could not be attributed to two friends having their fun in class.

As inconceivable as it may be to others, they took endless delight and humor in their under the radar communication. A cough here. A chair scoot there. A pencil sharpening to their predetermined speed or pace. Clearing the throat. The noises could be as subtle as breaking pencil lead or the squeak of an eraser. The noises were all mundane and untraceable to malfeasance of any sort.

So, they began their freshman year with another class together. English class. With Ms. Eberts. A dour faced adversary. Their favorite. As per their alphabetical lot, they were quite separated in class seating, which only made the challenge more enjoyable for them.

Cough

Andrew made an unassuming cough. David discretely covered his mouth and the smile underneath.

Mrs. Eberts droned on.

squeech, squeech... squeeech

David retorted with the pencil eraser noise. Highly practiced to elicit a humorous cadence.

Both Andrew and David were full of themselves. Another year of under the radar taunting had begun.

Mrs. Eberts droned on but tilted her head toward David.

Ever alert, David and Andrew made no sign of acknowledging her heightened awareness.

After class, they enjoyed a 2-minute exchange before going along their separate ways.

David snickered almost uncontrollably and punched Andrew.

"Dude, I thought she had us!" said David.

"No way. Her primate brain is perceptive but not able to cognitively process our codes," Andrew said with a laugh.

They high fived each other and went about their days.

The next day the two friends looked briefly at each other across the classroom. No words were necessary. A light grin briefly flickered across David's face. But then they were both the picture of studious freshmen. Nothing to distinguish them from the other 22 teenagers in the classroom of Ms. Sayrah Eberts.

Ms. Eberts was a private person. By almost any objective means, she was considered ugly. She was solidly built. Perhaps fat, but something about her implied a powerful, muscular build. Her usual stare was an almost far away indifference. Easy pickings for two cunning freshmen.

David led off with the classic fake cough. Nothing fancy. But a time tested, reliable opener.

Cough

Andrew let the prerequisite amount of time go by and volleyed with the phlegmatic throat clear.

Ahem

Ms. Eberts stopped talking. She turned on Andrew with a bird-like, predatory quickness.

"YOU BETTER STOP THAT FOOLISHNESS. I WON'T PUT UP WITH IT." Ms. Eberts voice exploded with power and bass.

Andrew was too surprised to do anything but gape at her like the other students. Ms. Eberts did not single out anyone, but she stabbed quick glances at both Andrew and then David, who was about to burst into uncontrollable silent laughter.

This justified a lengthy discussion. Andrew and David convened an evening war conference over the phone.

"How did she know it was fake? Everyone coughs and clears their throat at one time or another," asked David.

"I have no idea. Maybe I got sloppy. We've never been caught before," said Andrew.

They continued to discuss various strategies to employ.

"She has another think coming if she thinks she can shut us down," decreed David at the end of the call. The statement left Andrew with a funny feeling of dread, but he kept it to himself.

The boys decided to let some time go by. Better to be careful. They made note of the random classroom noises. They would be careful to ensure they were within the standard background noise and actions that occurred in the class. But there were other tricks up their sleeves.

David used the secret note technique. During a writing exercise, he was the third person to go use the pencil sharpener. He left an exceptionally compressed, tiny note on the adjoining shelf for Andrew to find. He could keep an eye on Ms. Eberts while he did so, and she was not looking in his direction. Time spent hiding note: perhaps a full second. Possibly less.

David returned to his seat and diligently began writing.

Later in the class, Andrew went to the pencil sharpener to retrieve the message. It was like the drop off, flawless and unseen.

Andrew returned to his seat.

"CLASS!" boomed Ms. Eberts. She looked around with no apparent focus in her gaze but pauses almost imperceptibly on Andrew—and then David—with a very brief, but withering, fierce glance. A look normally promising violence is not far away.

"IF I CATCH ANY OF YOU LEAVING NOTES, YOU **WILL** GET DETENTION."

This spooked Andrew and made David suspicious. They discussed it after school.

"It's just not possible she noticed us," said David on the phone.

"I know. But it happened," replied Andrew.

"Well, something isn't right about this. I'm going to do some homework on it."

Several days later, David called Andrew with his suspicions.

"OK. First of all, keep an open mind. Secondly, there may be nothing to this. We can test either theory," said David.

"Alright, alright! So, what did you find out?" asked Andrew.

"Well, I have two suspects. I'm not sure which is more likely or unlikely. The first one is that Ms. Eberts is a troll. Female trolls are not as identifiable as male trolls. They are often very human in appearance although most are considered plain, if not ugly."

"Check that box," said Andrew.

"They are also clever. And vindictive."

"Check that box," said Andrew.

"They possess the strength of 3-4 men. And while they are generally human in form, they have difficulty making their feet appear human. They sometimes have tails. They don't like sunlight at all."

Andrew couldn't help himself and said sarcastically, "Hey, Ms. Eberts, can you take your shoes off and lift up your skirt? Out here in the sunlight?"

"I know, I know. I'm only giving you the information," said David.

"Interesting. So, what's the other idea?" asked Andrew.

"This one is actually closely related to the first idea. It's just a bit more, uh, well, I'll let you make your mind up. Basically, some people think trolls are actually Neanderthal descendants."

Andrew met this idea with a blank look. "So... does that mean they are ugly humanoids or..."

"Or... both may be true," finished David. "I can test the troll theory, at least."

"How so?"

"Trolls do not like iron and steel. For example, you will notice Ms. Ebert's desk is wood, not metal."

"So..."

"So, we get close to her, and let me see if being in proximity to metal bothers her," said David. "There is one other thing, but I'm not sure if I can test it. When troll eyes encounter UV light, their eyes will reflect red. Sorta like a cat or deer in a flashlight except this is red. Maybe that's why her window shades in the classroom are always closed."

"Should we just leave her alone?" asked the more practical Andrew.

"Are you kidding me? Whether she is a troll or whatever, what have we done to her? Coughed in her class? No, she picked this fight, and we're going to finish it!" exclaimed David.

"I'm not so sure this is a good idea," said Andrew.

Three weeks later, David convinced Andrew enough time had passed. The school year was winding down.

squeak

David led off with the sole of his sneaker giving a squeak. Nothing major. But during the reading time, it was audible. But subtle.

cough, cough

Andrew retorted several minutes later with a faint double cough.

Nothing.

The end of class bell rang.

"Mr. David and Andrew, I would like a moment," said Ms. Eberts.

"Yes, ma'am?" asked Andrew with the utmost respect.

An uncomfortable silence followed.

"What am I to do with you two?" asked Ms. Eberts.

Another silence.

"WELL!" boomed Ms. Eberts.

"Ms. Eberts, what are you talking about?" asked David.

Ms. Eberts replied in a quiet, dangerous voice, "You know exactly what I'm talking about. And if you continue to insult my intelligence, I will start my own games with you two."

"I don't think that will be what you need to do. Or want to do," said David. "If you ask politely, I'm sure my friend and I can accommodate you. But if you want to be ugly about whatever is bothering you, I have some games to play myself. Games involving light and iron." David smirked, giving Andrew a sideways glance.

Another silence.

Andrew was shocked at the lack of response from Ms. Eberts.

"Mark my words carefully. I will not offer this again. Stay silent in my class unless called upon. Or you will regret it," said Ms. Eberts.

As she spoke, a cloud that had been covering the sun let the sunlight escape. While there was no direct sunlight, Andrew caught a glimpse of red in the teacher's eyes. It was a fleeting moment.

"Yes, ma'am" said David with respect.

The two boys left the classroom and talked later that night.

"So, let me get this straight. You think there is no doubt Ms. Eberts is a troll?" asked Andrew.

"I think the evidence is right in front of us. How can you deny it?"

"Well, for one, there was really nothing that was said that could prove it," replied Andrew.

"Light and iron?"

Andrew was troubled. In his heart, he suspected his friend was correct.

"She didn't even acknowledge that," he said halfheartedly.

David pressed, "Are you going to deny that you didn't see the red reflection in her eyes?"

"No. I saw it. What now?" asked Andrew.

David thought about it. "Well, sometimes it's best to just leave things well enough alone."

They did, but the encounter haunted them. There must be others.

Step On a Crack

Are there witches? Let me rephrase that. Are there witches who have actual power of some sort? Is it unreasonable to think there could be? Are curses sometimes effective? In this tale, the modern youth meets the modern witch.

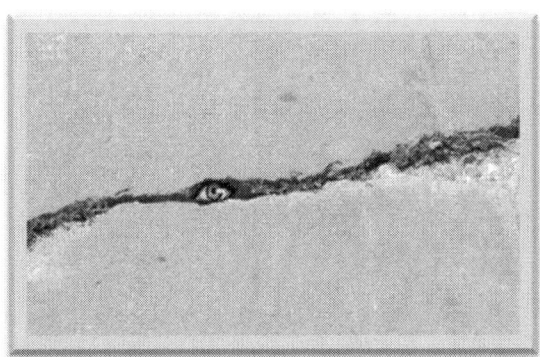

Alan was in a bad mood. Nothing unusual for an 18-year-old, but Alan seemed to possess a particularly nasty streak when he was in a bad mood. This time it was due to the usual suspects of grades and class attendance. Lost in his bitter thoughts, he almost did not hear the comment made by an old woman who appeared to be of very modest means.

"Step on a crack and break your mother's back," the old lady said in a friendly tone. Alan had just stepped on a crack in the sidewalk. Alan stopped and turned to see who had the temerity to interrupt his thoughts of self-pity.

"What did you say?" Comfortably upper-middle-class, Alan was disgusted as he examined the old lady's clothing. He went from being annoyed to furious.

"I was just saying..."

At almost 6 feet tall, Alan loomed over the old lady who was now visibly alarmed. Alan was pointing at her, and his finger was going up and down to emphasize each word. "Shut up, old lady! No one wants to hear what you think!"

The old lady looked up at Alan and raised both of her hands, palms up, trying to calm him down. "Young man..."

"Don't touch me, you hag! I don't want to catch one of your diseases!" yelled Alan as he shoved both of her hands down.

Alan turned and quickly stomped off, giving her no chance to reply. The old woman was humiliated and embarrassed. What was wrong with kids these days? Unfortunately for Alan, this old lady happened to be a real, albeit minor, witch.

"You will regret this, boy!"

Alan did not stop walking, but he did raise his middle finger and shook his head. The old lady's eyes narrowed. While she still had him in her sight, she began muttering an incantation. "Three times will you suffer for ignoring my friendly wives' tale. Only when you seek forgiveness will you be rid of the effects."

Within the hour, Alan got home and began looking around for a snack. Why couldn't his mother keep a steady supply of the *right* snacks for him? How could it be that hard? Alan was an only child and lived up to most of the stereotypes that go with it. He let out a slow breath. Only fruit? He promised himself he would give her the business about this matter when she got home. Until then, he helped himself to the apple and cubed watermelon.

He flopped down in front of the television and went into autopilot mode as he channel-surfed and ate his snacks. He did not even notice swallowing a few watermelon seeds.

~~~

It had been almost two weeks since his encounter with the old lady. The encounter that had not crossed his mind since it happened. He poked at his breakfast but was not hungry again.

"Mom, my stomach still hurts! The laxative you gave me worked but didn't stop the pain."

Alan's mother was rushing to get ready for work. Alan's father was already gone. She stopped and said, "Son, I'm sorry, but I have to go for now. Why don't you stay home? I'll make a doctor's appointment, and either your father or I will take you later. Will that work, Pooky?"

Alan rolled his eyes but secretly liked his mother's nickname for him. "Alright, Mom. Just hurry it up, will you? This hurts!"

Three hours later, Alan was waiting for the doctor to come into the room. He had been coming to see Dr. Philips for as long as he could remember. He used to think he was funny. Now he thought he was annoying and weird.

The door opened, and Dr. Phillips entered. He had read Alan's chart and made a silent wager with himself that Alan was faking to get out of school again.

"Well, hello there, Alan! I understand you have a stomachache, is that right?"

"Yes, Dr. Phillips, that's the problem."

Dr. Phillips began the normal routine of questions and poking around on Alan. He read the notes and was a bit surprised that the laxative did not work. While unlikely, there was a chance it could be something more serious.

"Alan, I tell you what. As a precaution, I would like to do a couple of x-rays, so we can see if there's any blockage or anything else going on that we need to know about. Nurse Jones here will take you where you need to go, and I'll see you in a bit."

Close to an hour later, Alan and his mother were talking with Dr. Phillips about the results of the x-ray. The conversation was winding down, and Dr. Phillips said, "As we have discussed, we can see that there is some sort of foreign object in your stomach Alan. Due to the vague shape and unknown nature of the object, I'm referring you to a specialist for an endoscopic procedure."

Alan and his mother left. Dr. Phillips took another look at the x-ray with a furrowed brow. The mass in Alan's stomach was too smooth and uniform to be a tumor. On the other hand, it appeared to be too large to have been swallowed.

~~~

Five days later, Dr. Phillips was visiting his patients at the hospital. He stopped in front of the next door and took a deep breath. He reread Alan's chart and shook his head. It was still hard to believe. Alan's pain had been caused by a watermelon that had taken root in his stomach and was growing. Until now, Dr. Phillips and the rest of the medical community had always considered this scenario to be one of the many wives' tales that modern medicine had disproved long ago. But he had seen the x-ray himself in the pictures of the postoperative procedure. Unlikely as it was, it happened.

Dr. Phillips opened the door and entered the room. Alan was in the first bed and awake. "Hello there, Alan! How are you doing this morning?"

"Whatever..." said Alan.

10 minutes later, Dr. Phillips left the room thinking to himself that the bizarre incident could not have happened to a more deserving teenager.

Miles away, the old witch gazed up into the sky and said to herself, "One."

~~~

Alan soon returned to his normal routine. The days passed by, and it was easier to rationalize what had happened with his surgery and revert to his normal behavior.

"Mom! How do you expect me to eat these eggs?" Alan was very particular about his eating habits, especially breakfast. Today his mother had not cooked his eggs to his particular and ever-changing standard.

"Alan, whatever do you mean?"

"Oh my God, Mother, do I really have to explain this?"

"Pooky! What's wrong now?"

Alan made his usual face behind his mother's back. It involved sticking out his tongue to the side of his mouth, frowning, crossing his eyes, and distorting his eyebrows. His mother turned around, and Alan was unable to revert to his normal facial expression quickly enough.

"Alan, why are you making that ugly face? Don't you know that if you do that it can get stuck that way?"

"Very funny, Mom!" After a few seconds, Alan came to the disturbing conclusion that he *could not* revert to a normal facial expression. Alan hurried to the restroom and examined himself in the mirror. He was not imagining this. Sure enough, his face was stuck. An incredulous panic, bit by bit, started to creep its way into his mind. Was this a face cramp? Was there even such a thing? He tried to massage the look from his face using his fingers. Nothing was working. This must be a freakish, momentary event that would stop at any moment. The minutes stretched on with no change.

"Alan, hurry up, or you will be late for school," said his mother as she turned the corner and saw him with the same expression on his face from earlier. "You really should not..."

"Mom. I don't think I will be going to school today."

~~~

Dr. Phillips studied Alan's chart. Alan and his mother had just left. Dr. Phillips was a rational man, a man of science. Alan's case did not sit well with him. First the bizarre watermelon incident. Now this frozen facial expression. His first suspicion was that Alan was seeking attention or otherwise trying to deceive everyone. The usual treatments had not made any changes. Not hydration. Not stretching. Not a heat compress. Not even a muscle relaxer, which was most disturbing of all.

Furthering his consternation; Alan seemed genuinely distressed and angry that he was exhibiting the facial expression. Of course, Alan seemed to be what may be described as a *problem* patient. Phillips was a Doctor of Medicine, not psychiatry. Hand on his chin, he considered the merits of the situation and decided to wait and see before recommending other courses of action.

Dr. Phillips sighed, shook his head, stood up, and left the room, thinking to himself that the bizarre incident could not have happened to a more deserving teenager.

Miles away the old witch looked up into the sky and said to herself, "Two."

~~~

Alan woke up and, for a few blissful seconds, forgot his dilemma. He felt no strain in his facial muscles, but he hurriedly got out of bed and stood in front of his mirror. Staring back at him was the face by and large reserved for the back of his mother's head. He was no better.

Alan was not introspective. He perceived himself as an intelligent young man of action and was not one to effectively analyze or evaluate his current circumstance. He stared back into his nonsensical reflection and gave a small sigh of resignation. Like a grazing animal, he did not understand why he did what he did or why he thrived or suffered. He strove to improve his position and, as a rule, took things as they were. Setbacks were the fault of others.

It was a warm Saturday morning. Alan cleaned up and went downstairs. His mother was doing something in the kitchen. Why was she always busying herself in the kitchen?

"Mom, do you have any breakfast for me?"

Alan's mother was rearranging some pots and a lower cabinet. She called back over her shoulder to Alan. "Well, good morning, sleepyhead! Any change today?"

"No change. How about that breakfast?"

"Pooky, I know you have been a little down about this situation, so I have some of your favorite bacon and cheese biscuits for you today!"

Alan's mother stood up and began to heat up the biscuits and prepare Alan's breakfast. He liked a small glass of orange juice and a 7 to 8-ounce glass of milk to go with his breakfast. She put an extra biscuit on his plate this morning. It might cheer him up to some degree.

"There you go, Alan! I hope you like your breakfast."

Without thanking his mother, Alan began to methodically consume his meal.

With food still in his mouth he asked his mother, "So where is Dad?"

"I asked him to go pick up a few things. He should be back in a couple of hours."

What to do today? Alan went over a checklist in his head. Most of his ideas involved going in public, which was not very appealing to him now. He might be able to hide his face with a hoodie or scarf in winter, but it was in the mid-80s, and that was not an option unless he wanted to be mistaken for a criminal. Perhaps exercise would help him. He decided to visit a neighbor's nearby pool.

"Mom, I think I'm going down to old lady Johansson's pool."

"Alan, you know better than to call her that! And it's very nice of her to allow you to swim whenever you want to."

Alan finished up his breakfast, leaving the mess he had made on the table for his mother to clean up. He was heading out of the room, and his mother called out to him, "Pooky, don't go swimming until your breakfast has had time to settle. Remember to always give yourself an hour, so that you don't get cramps or worse!"

"Okay, whatever."

~~~

The sun felt good. It was always relaxing to swim in old lady Johansson's pool. She was a widower and probably had a lot of money. The area around the pool was nicely landscaped. Today, this was a welcome escape for Alan. First, there was that stupid, freakish watermelon incident. Now his face was stuck in this comical expression. What had he done to deserve this? He was a great guy surrounded by idiots in his life. This just was not fair. The sun and water gradually took the edge off his mood, and he drifted leisurely around the pool, bobbing up and down in the water. The deep end was not too deep. At 8 feet (2.44 m) he could exhale, sink to the bottom, and bob up with little effort.

Alan took a breath, exhaled, and began his descent. He swiftly felt a pain in his stomach. Curling up made it worse. He tried to straighten back out and kicked to the surface, but now his muscles refused to cooperate. A stomach cramp! At first, he focused on the pain, but soon his focus reverted to an action he customarily took for granted. Breathing.

The struggle was over in a couple minutes. Alan let go of his breath. His struggling ceased, and he rotated by degrees in the water. He gazed up at the surface. There were some bubbles and the sun. The realization that he was drowning set in. As he faded out, he regretted not thanking his mother for the breakfast. Was he a bad person? If he was, at the end he was sorry.

Miles away the old witch looked up into the sky and said to herself, "Three."

~~~

No community liked having to bury a young person. Granted, Alan was not a popular boy, but his parents were liked well enough, and the turnout was respectable. The line at the viewing was long but moving along at a bearable pace. Dr. Phillips had heard about the tragic drowning. As he walked by the open casket, he noticed Allen's facial expression had reverted to a peaceful normalcy.

Looks like he was faking after all, thought Dr. Phillips to himself.

A couple of minutes later, an old lady walked by the casket. She kept a neutral expression but thought to herself, *it is a shame, but people by and large get what's coming to them—sooner or later.*

James Creek Bridge

Does your town have local legends? Urban legends? Do these indicate a part of our human nature? Do we have some sort of inherent need to create them? Or are these stories often based on facts? Would it be silly to believe all of them? On the other hand, would it be silly to discount every one of them? Let's take a look at a tale along those lines

October in the southeastern United States. Football season. Leaves changing. The mornings carry a welcome chill after the long summer. Halloween is just around the corner. In a suburb of Memphis, an unlikely friendship had been struck between Sadie and Patsy. Sadie was 8 years old (going on 9!) and enjoyed visiting her 80-year-old neighbor, Patsy. She felt a bit more dubious about Patsy's gruff husband, William. But he largely kept to himself, talking to the television most of the time.

Patsy painted and always had some sort of food around that Sadie loved. Sadie's mother liked seeing Sadie learn from her neighbor, who was a gracious and kindly vestige of a south that was fading with each passing year.

On this afternoon, Patsy had given Sadie some pumpkin pie, and they sat down on her covered back porch.

"Mrs. Patsy, do you like Halloween?"

"Well, I suppose I do. It wasn't such a big holiday when I was your age, but things were different back then," said Patsy in her sing-song voice. Patsy was gently rocking in her favorite chair. Her sweet tea rested on the coaster at her side.

"Did you ever see a ghost?"

"No, no," chuckled Patsy. "I never saw a ghost, but living in the country could be scary in other ways."

"I didn't know you grew up in the country! Where? Do you have any real scary stories?"

Patsy paused, and the smile left her face for a moment. "I suppose I do, but I don't know how scary it will seem to you. You must remember that back then we didn't have television and computers and these phones. Maybe it was easier to be scared."

"Well try me!" exclaimed Sadie. "Mama said supper wasn't until 6 o'clock tonight."

Patsy kept rocking and took a sip of her tea. "Well, there is one story I suppose has stuck with me. Just remember it was different back then. And I grew up in north Mississippi. Aberdeen. Close to Tupelo, where Elvis was born." A faraway look came to her eyes, and she began the story.

~~~

Patsy grew up on a farm outside of Aberdeen, Mississippi. Long before Mississippi was a state, her home was the home of the Chickasaw Native American tribe. Patsy was young in the 1940s when the stories from the Chickasaw were not so easily dismissed as simple tales. The modern world had the luxury of distance to evaluate these stories, and the verdict was usually *fable*.

But in the 1940s, there were not many generations of separation from the time when settlers were few and far between. Not all relations with the Indians, as they were called then, were unfriendly. The settlers often traded with different Chickasaw families. They also had a window of time to directly hear the tribal lore and legends. Soon the tribe would be gone, but some stories would live on. As the years went by and civilization increased its hold on the area, the stories were generally regarded as myth. But the settlers did not convey some stories as myths. This was one of those stories.

Countless moons ago, long before the stranger Desoto passed through their territory, the Chickasaw enjoyed abundant hunting along the western tributaries of the Tombigbee River. The creeks feeding into the river were well populated with deer, bear, and wild turkey. For countless years, the tribe had figured out the best grazing and watering points to hunt.

While they would sometimes fish, they were wary of the dark waters. A Great Serpent lived in the waters and would steal game from the hunters who were returning home as they crossed a creek. If they denied the Serpent, it had been known to take a warrior instead. Over time the Chickasaw learned it was better to appease the Serpent rather than trying to deny it. They would throw choice game parts into the waters before crossing. This arrangement lasted for ages.

In 1808, the renowned Chickasaw leader Tishominko was hunting game along one of the creeks. He had just killed and field dressed a large buck close to the creek. The Great Serpent approached him at the edge of the water.

Tishominko spoke. "Father Serpent, I offer you this fine deer, but I also give you a warning. The White People are coming, and they will not honor our arrangement. We have always respected you and come to a peace. But they have strange weapons and powers that I fear will overcome you."

"I have seen many of your kind come and go. Thank you for your respect and advice, but I will adapt to them as well," replied the Serpent.

"Father Serpent, I hope what you say is true, but I think change has come to the world, and things will not be as they are now. Heed my warning when we are gone."

The Great Serpent's eyes seemed to glow as he took the deer back into the water.

And it came to pass that Tishominko was correct. The Chickasaw were forced to leave in the 1830s. For a time, the Serpent had the creeks to himself. But the settlers started to make roads and houses. They were no longer just passing through. And they offered the Great Serpent nothing.

Soon stories began circulating in the area. Missing dogs. Mules drowning. Particularly in what was now known as James Creek, a nice hunting area. One or two of the old-timers recalled the words of Tishominko. He had asked the whites to respect the spirit in the waters. But the settlers were not given to superstition, at least not publicly. But something had to be done when a young man hunting in the area disappeared without a trace. A meeting was held at a nearby church. It did not take long to form an agreement to build a bridge. Officially, one man died during the construction. The official cause of death was drowning although no body was ever found.

The years rolled by. The bridge was rebuilt and improved to a covered bridge. The road was upgraded and known as "Darracott Road" as it linked Aberdeen in the north with Darracott crossroads to the south.

A cloud hung over the James Creek Bridge. People sometimes disappeared in the area, but they were always alone and proving the circumstances of their demise was not possible. Rumors persisted that mules and horses were not safe crossing the bridge after sundown. There was one group of people who were not afraid of being superstitious. The African Americans, known as colored people at that time, refused to cross the bridge at night. As cars became more common, people were not as scared to cross the bridge at night, but it became customary to honk the horn as you arrived. To scare... something away.

So it was when a young Patsy in the 1940s grew up just down the road from the bridge. Her family had a farm that went as far as the north side of the creek. She would find arrowheads in the fields close to the creek, a testament to the richness of the old hunting ground. But she was warned to never swim in or cross the creek. It was too dangerous. Why? Well, you could drown, of course! But as Patsy reached the age of 11, she began to hear and recall more than drowning stories and warnings. What was she to make of it all? She decided to ask her father.

Patsy's father was a kindhearted but no-nonsense farmer. Patsy approached him one afternoon in late October. "Daddy, why do some people warn about crossing the bridge at night?"

Edward, her father, looked at her sharply. "Who's been telling you about the bridge?" he asked.

"Well, Daddy, I guess I've heard several people say things. Is there anything to fear?"

"You just listen to what I've always told you, and don't cross the creek. Bridge or not. Unless I'm taking you. Do you understand?" Edward asked with an uncommon firmness.

"Yes, sir," replied Patsy.

"You got no business down there unless I'm with you. And that's that." And so that was the end of that. For the time being, anyway. The 40s and 50s rolled by, and the covered bridge was replaced with a modern steel and cement bridge. Patsy went away and married a young man from Atlanta. The tumultuous 60s came and went. It was in the middle of the 70s that brought the next chapter to the bridge.

Patsy returned to her parent's home whenever she could with her children. The oldest was a son, well behaved and compliant. His name was Robert. Even at the young age of 14, he was akin to a reborn John Wesley, in demeanor and intellect. The middle child, also a son, was often not so well behaved. His name was David, and he liked to explore and push boundaries. It was not that he was mean or evil. No, he just liked to *push* life. Even at the age of 12. It would be fair to say he was a bit Tom Sawyer-ish. The youngest child, Catherine, was a 2-year-old. Patsy's parents were semi-retired now. She thought that time on the farm was good for children even if things were not as austere as they were when she was growing up.

On this 5-day summer trip, only David and Catherine were in tow. And David's friend, Andrew. The eldest son, Robert, was attending a youth musicians camp for the gifted, and David complained bitterly until convincing Patsy to bring his friend. David's friend Andrew was an interesting and good-natured friend. He made excellent grades and was normally a well-behaved young man. But like a moth to a flame, Andrew was always getting drawn into David's misadventures.

After a day to settle in, Edward presented a plan to Patsy and the boys.

"You know, I've been trying to figure out what to do with an old wagon out by the barn. What do you boys say we make a treehouse out of it? If Patsy will agree to it, of course." Edward has a sparkle in his eye. He enjoyed seeing how the boys became excited almost instantly.

"Daddy, I don't mind, but remember we're only here for a few more days," said Patsy.

"Well, that shouldn't be a problem. I rounded up some materials last week on a trip to town. We should be able to have it up and going in a day or two."

"Where are you going to put it?" asked Patsy.

"I believe there are two trees just about the right distance apart on the south pasture edge," said Edward. "I'll raise the wagon with the front-end loader, and it will be half made already."

Patsy nodded her head. She knew the hill her father was referencing. It was on the way toward James Creek but not so close she would worry too much.

Andrew, who had not been listening closely, asked, "How are we going to put a wagon up in a tree?"

David punched him in the arm and said, "We're going to put it between two trees! Get the mud out of your ears!"

"David! Don't you treat your guest like that! You apologize right now!" said Patsy.

David groaned and mumbled a halfhearted apology to Andrew, who mockingly grinned back at his friend.

Edward stood and said, "Well, we better rest up, boys. This will take a lot of work. Time to hit the hay!"

Two days later, the tree house was complete. It was quite the structure! David proposed moving into it permanently, but Patsy told him he would have to convince his father before he could do that. David dropped the proposal. His father was rarely intrigued with David's ongoing theories and adventures. He did, however, convince his mother to let Andrew and himself to spend the night in the treehouse.

Spirits were high through supper and while they moved their things into the treehouse for a night in the wilderness. Well, to David it was wilderness—at least for the night. It was only about ½ a mile to the treehouse, but as Edward drove away in his truck, the boys felt a bit less lighthearted. But that feeling passed when David proposed a wilderness expedition. As usual, Andrew was swept along in his friend's plan, which always sounded fun, at least when they started.

"Alright, let's move out!" said David. Andrew dutifully complied. They were both laden with their expedition gear—canteens, knives, flashlights, snacks, walking sticks. They were prepared.

It was not complete darkness yet. It was the dark blue time after sunset but not quite full evening. Summer days seemed to drag out the process. The boys made their way along the fence line, shining their lights into the woods. Cicadas droned on. The heat of the day was gone with the daylight.

"What are we looking for?" asked Andrew.

"Anything! We're explorers!" said David.

"Oh, yeah. I almost forgot," said Andrew, perhaps sardonically.

The boys traipsed on. Time seemed suspended as the two friends kept up their Lewis & Clark personas, shining their lights frequently into the woods with periodic, whispered dialogue. Before they knew it, they had drifted down the hill leading to the creek.

"I've never been this far," said David to himself as they came to a new fence.

"Do you hear water?" asked Andrew.

"Yeah, James Creek is just over there, and I think I can make out where the old bridge used to be," said David. They both shined their lights in the direction of the creek. Two red eyes peered back at them. They froze. A huge snake or dragon creature suddenly loomed over them. The two parties stared at the other.

+Inquiry+ said the Great Serpent in an incongruent artificial voice.

David could only muster a, "Huh?"

Andrew could not muster a reply.

+Inquiry. Maintenance standby mode. Render assistance or face consequences+ said the Serpent.

"Uh, OK. What do you want us to do?" asked David. Andrew could only stare, mouth agape.

+Is your companion damaged+ inquired the Serpent.

"I don't think so. He just gets nervous sometimes."

+Very well. We will proceed.+

Roughly a half hour later, David and Andrew had completed the tasks that the Serpent had given them.

"Thank you for your service," said the Great Serpent, in a new, deep, raspy, and imposing voice—a voice the Chickasaws would have recognized.

"Yes, sir," said David. "So, who are you?"

"I am unit **+00100110101110001+** but you may refer to me as Scout 7. I have been on assignment in this area for 3,861 of your years. My pickup was delayed due to the maintenance you assisted with. My self-maintenance routines could not fully compensate for this humidity over time."

"Well. OK. Glad we could help," said David. The time span was incomprehensible to him.

"Where are you from? China?" asked Andrew. This drew a sharp glance from David, but Scout 7 replied.

"I am from elsewhere, and now I can return. And now you will leave," said the Serpent, in a matter-of-fact manner. The boys backed off, and the Serpent watched them leave with his glowing red eyes.

The dumbfounded boys stumbled back to the treehouse. There was little conversation on the way back to the perceived safety of the treehouse. They returned and cleaned up. Soon they were sitting, reviewing events in hushed tones. A pale blue glow casting shadows in the interior of the tree house froze them.

Back at the house, Patsy had put Catherine down for bed and was looking out the window toward the treehouse.

Edward chuckled. "Now, Patsy, don't you worry. At the first sign of trouble, I'm sure they will be knocking on the door. And I'll get up early to check on them." He kissed her on the cheek and went off to prepare for bed with her mother.

Patsy lingered by the window. Her attention was complete when a pale blue column of light seemed to rise from the creek. There was no noise. It just kept going up. And then it was gone.

The next morning, David and Andrew told Patsy about the encounter. She saw the blue light herself but was not sure what to say. The boys were still young, and David could be mischievous at times. Was he telling the truth? She tells them that the creek has always been a place of strange occurrences and that maybe the story was best kept between them.

Years later, Patsy had plenty of time to think about the history of the area and David's story. Could it be true? Was there some sort of scout that had been in the area that long? Scouting? For whom? Was it the cause of the missing animals and people? Why? *Dissection?* Was it gone or still there? Patsy did not like the possible answers to her questions.

~~~

Patsy finished up and said, "So that is that. What do you think, Ms. Sadie?"

Sadie did not know what to think. She simply said, "Mrs. Patsy, that is no boring country story. Was it real or made up?"

"Oh, I'm not one to make things up." She let out a quiet laugh. "But you think what you want to. I thought you might enjoy that with Halloween coming up. And now, let me give you a souvenir," said Patsy as she stood up and went over to one of her sewing drawers.

"Ah, here we go. You take this home with you. It is real. And if you ever get grown up and curious, go see the James Creek Bridge on Darracott Road for yourself."

Sadie kept it for the rest of her life. A real arrowhead! In later years, it made her think more about the story and just how much truth was in it. And if there was still something scouting around James Creek.

Epilogue

Several years later there was a severe and extended summer drought in that part of the country. It was worse than any drought the oldest residents could recall. The water level in all the lakes, rivers, and creeks dropped. James Creek was no exception.

And so it was that a surveyor who had been hired by the county to do a survey of the area stumbled upon something that at any other time would have been out of sight. On one side of the bank near the creek bed, far below the normal water line, was a sizable hole. Out of curiosity, he ventured down and squeezed into the opening, which was clearly the beginning of what was not a natural formation. He continued down for perhaps 50 yards. At that point, it took a quick upward turn that ended in a large cavern with open air. Not wanting to venture further, he noted the location and relayed the information to a friend who worked in the geology department of a local university, not too many miles away.

Further investigation by the friend and a couple of colleagues revealed the presence of a large assortment of skeletal remains, both animal and human, which were spread out in a loosely organized fashion. They returned soon after with a team of forensic scientists from the FBI. Along with the bones, they found several violent-looking implements that resembled medical instruments. And strangest of all, the instruments were composed of an alloy that could not be, and has never been, identified.

Bottom Feeder

This is the first modest attempt at a sequel. But it also considers the idea that alien visitors may not consider land animals the most interesting things to study.

The ship remained in low orbit, undetected by the primitive land dwellers.

+Extraction Successful- Scout 7 retrieved+ said the co-pilot.

+Proceed to primary mission - individual behavioral analysis+ announced the pilot.

The alien craft descended to an unsuspecting Earth.

I love sleeping. Brod thought to himself before falling back to sleep.

Quiet, sleepy. Brod drifted in and out of sleep again.

What's that smell? Brod asked himself. Oh well... maybe later. More sleep.

That smells delicious... God I'm starving, thought Brod.

Do I have to get out of bed?

Oh well, I'm hungry.

Brod got out of bed and conducted minimal grooming before leaving. *I hate going out like this.* He approached the new eatery. *Ugh! Crowds are awful. Everyone is rude.*

"Excuse me," Brod blurted out to no one in particular. *Oh well, I gotta eat, crowds or not.* Brod was careful. You never knew who you might offend at these new places.

Ah, why do I always do this to myself? I always overeat. I'm not even sure what I just ate! Some of it was soft, some crunchy. Why do I overeat? I can hardly move now.

Suddenly, a blinding light assaulted Brod's senses.

Ahhh!! Run away!

Brod scurries off as fast as he can. Most of the others do not react.

~~~

+These organisms are violent and gluttonous. So unlike our water home+ stated the pilot.

+Changing to light spectrum range to 100-700 nanometers+ said the co-pilot.

+Very little reaction. A few creatures instinctively fled+ commented the co-pilot.

The pilot consulted the data records and decided. **+We misplaced our hopefulness. These creatures are no better** than the primitive land dwellers; they just pollute less of their environment+

The pilot and co-pilot began preparing to leave the planet. Perhaps Scout 7 would offer some hope for intelligence evolving to a level that would merit contact.

~~~

Ahh. Sleep again.

Brod settled in after his harrowing experience. He resented having to run with such a full stomach. Who would do such a thing? Dead whales were not common, and there were edible tissues aplenty.

Brod burrowed back into the mud. Time for more sleep. Perhaps for months. One never knew. 30-inch long Giant Isopods have low metabolisms.

Dream Amulet

What if you knew what was going to happen to people you knew? Would you warn them? What if you were not always correct? Do many of us think we already have such a power through our wisdom? In this tale we explore a case in which someone literally gets more than they bargained for.

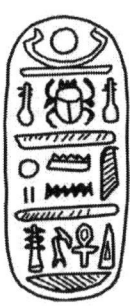

Bart Willington fans himself with his hat. Sweat pours from his head. His wife and kids have stayed at the hotel after the heat they encountered the day before. But with only 2 days left on their trip to Egypt, Bart wants to pick up a unique souvenir.

Bart pays the guide from the hotel to take him to some street-side shops. He does not speak their incomprehensible language and does not care for many of their sullen looks. Yes, he is a poster boy for the condescending American abroad.

"Khalid! Boy! How soon until we get there?"

The boy chafes slightly at the insulting tone, but he will be making good money from the errand, which should not take too long.

"Ustad," the skinny, native boy replies with the polite title for a man similar to sir, "just a few minutes. We are almost there."

Bart resigns himself to more misery and keeps walking. He is glad to have seen the Pyramids in Giza, but the surrounding city and culture are bewildering and not to his liking. His senses are almost overwhelmed with the noises, smells, and sights of the Giza streets. He misses the insulation of driving in his car.

With the turn of a corner, they arrive at the street of vendors. A timeless sight! Vendors hock goods of all sorts. Buyers drive for bargains. Everyone is gesticulating. The cluck of chickens, bleating of goats, and the babble of humanity serve as background noise. Most people would be enchanted with the sight. Not Bart.

"Good Lord," he mutters to himself.

"Ustad, what sort of shop would you like?" asks Khalid.

"Ah, well. I suppose a place with bracelets or amulets would do. Something of that nature."

Several minutes later, he is in front of a storefront on the sidewalk. The seller dons a loose-fitting, ankle-length robe. A skullcap covers his head. He speaks quickly to the boy in a cadence belying impatience. The boy converses with him, and suddenly the storekeeper's countenance brightens. Soon they are finished speaking. *Oh great. The boy probably told him I'm a rich American and to stick it to me.*

"Ustad, the shopkeeper's name is Jabari, and he would be pleased to show you his merchandise," says Khalid.

"I'm sure," mutters Bart.

Soon enough, an amulet catches Bart's eye.

"What is this?" he asks. He points to a circular pendant of what appears to be a bluish crystal, with an eye inscribed on it.

Through Khalid, Jabari explains that it was a dream charm. The bearer will have visions of the future for himself and the people he knows—for a low price of 200EG£ (Egyptian Pounds).

Bart rolls his eyes, so that the Egyptians can see his contempt.

"Khalid. Please tell Mr., ah, Jabari that I am not a simpleton, and there is no need to create a false sense of value in this trinket. I will pay 65EG£ and no more. Now, if he will stop all the incessant bantering and take my offer, we can conclude our business. Otherwise, I will find another place."

Bart is aware that he is offering enough to buy a gallon of milk. The amulet appears to be well made, so he thinks he is getting a good value.

The boy did not completely understand everything Bart had told him, but he understands the main points and dutifully conveys them to Jabari.

The vendor has experienced this every so often with these foreign buyers. Normally he takes it in stride, but today he is more annoyed. Perhaps it is the manner of this buyer more than anything.

Jabari quickly agrees to sell the amulet at the dictated price, but unbeknownst to the arrogant and gleeful Bart, the vendor has decided to inscribe a hieroglyphic jinx on the amulet. He does so behind his curtain, where he wraps and prepares his sales.

Bart returns home with his family. Home! The land of air conditioning and drive-through coffee! He puts the amulet on his nightstand and gets back into the grind of his corporate life.

Eight days later, there is a full moon. Bart is unaware of it. He is, however, very aware of a dream he experiences that night.

Bart dreams that he is in front of a hospital. Bart hates hospitals as they always reminded him of death. He wonders what he is doing in front of the hospital, wearing a suit instead of the pajamas he slept in. Bart finds this dream very strange as he discovers the suit he is currently wearing was what he is meant to wear to work for a presentation in three days' time. He wonders if this were his mind's way of telling him that he would do well at the presentation.

"Are you Mr. Willington?" a young lady in a nurse outfit asks hastily as she comes out of the hospital building.

Bart is rather startled as he has been lost in his own thoughts.

"Yes, I am. Why are you asking?" Bart asks.

"Your friend, Mr. Bob Foster, needs you inside before we pull the plug," the nurse says with doleful eyes.

"What plug, and how did you know my name?" Bart asks. *Does she have me mixed up with someone else?*

"I understand that you must be upset, but you need to come with me right now. He does not have much time left." The nurse says before going back into a hospital doorway.

Bart stands in shock as he watches the retreating figure of the nurse. She had sounded like a lunatic. Bob is quite healthy.

Bart is torn between just standing where is or following the nurse. He wonders if his friend Bob was really in the hospital and finally decides to follow.

The smell of antiseptic greets him as he opens the door and enters a waiting room filled with people with different injuries and ailments. Bart sees a man with a group of nurses around him as they put him on a stretcher. Bart looks away immediately as he discovers that he is already feeling faint. This is another reason why he hates hospitals. He cannot stand the sight of blood.

Where did that nurse go? Bart realizes the nurse is no longer there. He follows a sign to the nurse station to see if they can help him out.

"Hi." Bart glances at his watch to check the time before he continues with his greeting. "Could you point me to the nurse with a red bow in her brown hair?" Bart inquires.

"Good evening. If you have a health emergency, fill this form," the nurse says in a robotic voice without looking up.

"I'm simply asking for directions," Bart says curtly.

"It's you, Mr. Willington, sorry about that," the nurse says apologetically as she withdraws the form she had pushed towards him.

Bart was starting to get creeped out. *How did she know his name?*

"What did you say you wanted? Nurse Chiu has been looking for you. Have you seen her yet?"

Bart can only assume that the nurse he had met outside the hospital was Nurse Chiu.

"Not really," Bart says, lying. "Could you point me in the direction that she went?'

"She is with Mr. Foster. They have all been waiting for you," says the nurse. She glances at her computer screen twice to indicate that she wants to go back to work.

Bart hesitates before speaking. "Please, could you tell me what room that is?"

"Are you sure you are OK, Mr. Willington?" The nurse looks at Bart as if he is losing his mind.

"I can't just think properly right now," Bart says in a sad voice. He hopes that would make the nurse believe him.

"It's fine. They are in the last room before the emergency ward."

Bart still looks confused.

"There is a map by that wall," the nurse says, pointing to a wall.

"Thank you," Bart says before going to the wall. He crams the direction into his head before stepping into the elevator.

Bart finds Nurse Chiu by the door of a room, and she looks at him impatiently.

"What is going on with you, Mr. Willington?" she asks.

"I think I'm just tired," Bart says.

"Sorry about that. I know this must be awfully hard for you, but Mr. Foster really wants you to be here before the plug is pulled." She places her hand on the door handle. *Plug is pulled? Since when do health professionals use that term?*

Bart stops her before she opens the door. "Please stop," Bart says in a shaky voice. He does not understand why he has become so emotional. Now he is not sure if he is ready to find out what is behind the door.

"Mr. Willington, we really can't keep delaying this whole process. You need to be strong for your friend," Nurse Chiu says sympathetically as she opens the door.

Bart finds the ground move beneath his feet as he looks at his friend. Bob is hooked to a life machine and looks very pale. Bart notices that his feet begin to move on their own accord to where his friend was. He knew he needed to wake up from whatever dream this was.

"Bob, it's me," Bart says as he moves closer to him.

"I was wondering if you were going to make it in time," Bob says.

Bart cannot believe what he was seeing. "What happened, Bob? How did you get here?" Bart says in a cracked voice. He is trying hard not to break into tears.

"Bart, I shouldn't have gone for that fundraiser. But I went, and a drunk driver hit my car. Be strong for me Bart. I believe I am ready to go now," Bob says as the sound of the monitor begins to beat rapidly. Bob's eyes gently close, and the monitor becomes silent.

"What just happened?" Bart asks frantically. He feels like he is on a reality show, and he cannot wait for the joke to be over.

Nurse Chiu just looks at Bart sadly as she checks the time and scribbles something down.

"What exactly are you writing down, don't just stand there. Call the doctor!" Bart exclaims.

"No, he is not dead!" Bart shouts.

"What is going on with you, Bart?" a gentle voice calls out to Bart, but he is unable to open his eyes. He does not want to face a world without his friend.

"Bart, you're scaring me," the voice calls out again.

Bart opens his eyes slowly, expecting to see Nurse Chiu hovering his head to confirm his fear. Instead, it is his wife who was doing that. She has a worried expression on her face.

"How is Bob?" Bart asks.

"Bob is fine. He actually left you a message," she says.

"So. Bob is fine… It was just a stupid dream," Bart says as he begins to chuckle.

"What sort of dream did you have? You practically woke up sweating like you just ran a marathon."

"It was nothing dear," Bart says before kissing his wife on the cheek and going into the bathroom. Bart brushes his teeth when he enters the bathroom and goes ahead to take a quick shower when he notices that he is sweaty.

Bart comes out of the bathroom a few minutes later and decides to play the message Bob had left him; his heart began to beat rapidly for no reason.

"I just got an extra ticket to this fundraiser event. Do you think you can make it?" Bob says in the voice message.

The wheels on Bart's head begin to turn. *Fundraiser.... Is that not what he went for that got him killed in my dream? Nah, it must be a coincidence.* Bart thinks to himself as he grabs his phone.

The phone rings twice before Bob picks it up.

"What took you so long to call? You would not believe what is going on right now." Bob says in an alarmed voice.

"What is happening?" Bart asks worriedly.

"Hey! Lighten up! I was just joking. Hey, can you go to a fundraiser soon? Sorry for springing this up on you last minute."

"No, I don't think so. I don't think I have a suit ready," Bart says.

"I assumed you were going to say that. I already sent a suit to you, and it should be arriving any minute now," Bob says. "I have to go now; Nancy wants to try out another dress."

"OK, bye," Bart says as the call ends. He goes to meet his wife downstairs.

"Bart, a suit just came in for you. I could swear that it looks like the one you have in your closet. Did you make a mistake of ordering two identical suits?" Bart's wife says as she examines the suit in her hands.

Bart stops in his tracks as he feels quite sure that his dream is foretelling what is going to happen.

Bart immediately picks up his phone and calls Bob. He begs Bob not to go to the fundraiser event, but Bob laughs him off.

On the day of the fundraiser, Bart tries to head off Bob from going to the fundraiser. If necessary, he will flatten a tire. He encounters traffic on his way and is delayed for an extra hour before he finally arrives at Bob's house. Bob has already left for the fundraiser.

Bart heads home. He receives a call from Bob's wife, Nancy. Bob is in the hospital.

Bart finds himself shaken as he rushes to the hospital. When he gets to the hospital, he discovers it was the same one he had seen in his dream. Bart breaks down totally when he sees Nurse Chiu. He knows what will happen next and just drives home. He is not going to watch his friend die again.

A few days after Bob's burial, another full moon appears. Bart dreams again. This time he dreams about his co-worker Tom, whose wife is cheating on him. When Tom finds out that his wife is cheating on him, they go through a messy divorce, which results in Tom being penniless at the end of the divorce.

Remembering how his other dream went, Bart tells Tom that his wife is cheating and begs him not to divorce her. Tom tells him to mind his own business. Through the ensuing conversation, it is strongly implied that Tom is not only aware of the affair, but he is also okay with it. Needless to say, this damages their friendship.

Bart is confused. How did he get it wrong? The dream was clear.

The next full moon arrives, and he dreams again. This time he dreams that his uncle will have a heart attack alone at his home and die. Bart reluctantly does nothing about it. 10 days later his uncle dies. Just as he had dreamed. Bart feels very guilty and begins to feel cursed.

Bart dreams every full moon, and when he tells people about it, it usually makes things worse. He feels like he is losing his sanity, and his marriage is now under severe strain.

Bart racks his memory and recalls when all his problems began. Egypt. The strange man who had sold him the amulet. He had not believed when the man had told him it was a dream charm but was starting to do so now. He picks up the amulet from his dressing table and looks at it curiously. He could not believe such a little thing could be the cause of all his troubles.

Disturbed by the amulet, Bart sells it on eBay. He sells it at a cheap price, but he does not mind. All he cares about is getting the amulet out of his house.

The next day the amulet finally leaves Bart's house. Bart is humbler after being haunted by the revealed futures and scorned severely by people he misinformed. Now he lives every dreamless month with a feeling of gratitude. He no longer dreams the prophetic dreams, but he is often haunted by the what-ifs of his actions after the dreams.

The next month, it is a full moon in Denver. A college student named Sierra rolls over on her bed, lost in a dream as her new amulet sits comfortably on her bed stand.

More by A.P. Simmons

Please visit the website of A.P. Simmons for this and other books!

https://www.apsimmons.com/

Made in the USA
Las Vegas, NV
19 December 2021